A Robbie Reader

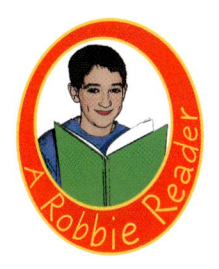

Albert Einstein
SCIENCE GENIUS

by
Susan Zannos and
Jamie Kondrchek

Mitchell Lane
PUBLISHERS

P.O. Box 196
Hockessin, Delaware 19707
Visit us on the web: www.mitchelllane.com
Comments? email us: mitchelllane@mitchelllane.com

Mitchell Lane PUBLISHERS

Copyright © 2005 by Mitchell Lane Publishers. All rights reserved. No part of this book may be reproduced without written permission from the publisher. Printed and bound in the United States of America.

Printing 1   2   3   4   5   6   7   8   9

A Robbie Reader

Hillary Duff
Philo T. Farnsworth
Mia Hamm
Donovan McNabb

Thomas Edison
Henry Ford
Tony Hawk
Dr. Seuss

Albert Einstein
Robert Goddard
LeBron James
Charles Schulz

Library of Congress Cataloging-in-Publication Data
Zannos, Susan and Jamie Kondrchek.
   Albert Einstein / by Susan Zannos and Jamie Kondrchek.
       p. cm. — (A Robbie reader)
   Includes bibliographical references and index.
       ISBN 1-58415-305-9 (lib. bdg.)
   1. Einstein, Albert, 1879-1955—Juvenile literature. 2. Physicist—Biography—Juvenile literature. I. Title. II. Series.
   QC16.E5Z36 2005
   530'.092--dc22

2004009299

ABOUT THE AUTHOR: Susan Zannos has been a lifelong educator, having taught at all levels, from preschool to college, in Mexico, Greece, Italy, Russia, and Lithuania, as well as in the United States. She has published a mystery *Trust the Liar* (Walker and Co.) and *Human Types: Essence and the Enneagram* (Samuel Weiser). Her book, *Human Types,* was recently translated into Russian, and in 2003 Susan was invited to tour Russia and lecture about her book. Another book she recently completed, *Careers in Education* (Mitchell Lane), was selected for inclusion in the New York Public Library's "Books for the Teen Age 2003 List." She has written nearly twenty books for children and young adults, including *Chester Carlson and the Development of Xerography* and *The Life and Times of Franz Joseph Hayden* (Mitchell Lane). When not travelling, Susan lives in the Sierra Foothills of Northern California.
Jamie Kondrchek is a student studying English at the University of Delaware. She has worked in publishing part-time for the past five years and hopes to be a full-time editor when she graduates.
PHOTO CREDITS: p. 4: Hulton-Deutsch Collection/Corbis; p. 6 Austrian Archives/Corbis; p. 8 Photo Researchers; p. 10 Leo Baeck Institute/Archive Photos; p. 12: Getty; p. 14 Topical Press Agency/Getty; p. 16 Underwood & Underwood/Corbis; p. 18 AP Photos; p. 20 Keystone/Getty; p. 22 Underwood & Underwood/Corbis; p. 24 American Stock/Getty; p. 25 Globe Photos; p. 26 MPI/Getty
ACKNOWLEDGMENTS: The following story has been thoroughly researched, and to the best of our knowledge, represents a true story. While every possible effort has been made to ensure accuracy, the publisher will not assume liability for damages caused by inaccuracies in the data, and makes no warranty on the accuracy of the information contained herein.

TABLE OF CONTENTS

Chapter One
Growing Up 5

Chapter Two
A Bad Student 9

Chapter Three
Hard Times 15

Chapter Four
Fame 19

Chapter Five
Going to America 23

Chronology 28
Find Out More 29
Glossary 31
Index 32

This is a photo of Albert and his sister, Maja. When they were young children, they did not get along very well. Once they grew up, they became very good friends.

CHAPTER ONE

GROWING UP

In Ulm Germany, a couple named Hermann and Pauline Einstein became very worried on the day of March 14, 1879. Their first son had just been born. They could already see he was different from other newborn babies. The baby's head was a funny shape and he was very big. "Much too fat!" Grandma cried. Hermann and Pauline named their new son Albert.

When Albert was a young child, he did not like to talk very much. If he did speak, he said strange things. His parents were afraid he was not very smart.

"Soon you will have a baby sister to play with," his mother told Albert one day. When he

CHAPTER ONE

Albert learned to play the violin at a young age. He continued to play as he got older.

saw his baby sister, Albert said, "Where are the wheels?" He thought his sister Maja (MAH-jah) would be a toy with wheels.

At home, Albert had a bad temper. Albert's mother noticed that Albert enjoyed watching her play the piano. She thought he would be good at playing an instrument, so she hired a violin teacher for Albert and Maja. At the first lesson, Albert threw a chair at his violin teacher. The teacher did not come back. His mother got a braver teacher and soon Albert learned to play.

Maja, Albert's little sister, learned to be careful of her older brother's temper. Once Albert was so mad that he hit Maja with a garden hoe. Maja noticed when Albert was mad, his face turned white. Maja would know to run and hide.

Soon Albert calmed down. He and Maja became very good friends for the rest of their lives.

A young, college-aged Albert sits here. He did not like school very much.

CHAPTER TWO

A BAD STUDENT

Albert did not start school until he was seven years old. His teachers said he was slow. The other children thought he was boring because he did not like sports. None of them wanted to play with Albert.

Albert never did well in school. He only liked to study math. He enjoyed asking difficult questions about science and math and finding the answers to those questions. But he did not like to do the work in the classroom.

When Albert was 15, his family moved to Italy and left Albert behind to finish school. After high school, he would also have to serve in the army before he could leave Germany. Albert lived alone in a rented room. He was

CHAPTER TWO

Albert enjoyed asking difficult questions about science and math and finding the answers to those questions.

A BAD STUDENT

very sad. His teachers did not like him and he had no friends. Albert hated his school and wanted to be with his family.

Albert convinced his doctor that he was sick. He said he needed to quit school to live with his family. The doctor wrote a letter to Albert's school. Albert took the letter to the principal. The principal let Albert drop out of school and go to Italy.

Albert was happy to be with his family again, but his parents were disappointed that he had dropped out of school. He liked Italy and made friends. But there was a big problem. He did not **graduate** high school. He could not go to a **university** and nobody wanted to hire him for a job.

Albert found out about a school in Switzerland that accepted students based on an entrance exam, not whether they had finished high school or not. Albert's father decided it was a good idea. Albert did not pass the

CHAPTER TWO

Albert made a sneaky plan to quit high school so he could live with his family in Switzerland.

entrance exam, but his math scores were very high. The school was impressed with these scores. The school said Albert could go to the school but he had to wait until the next year. Until then, he had to return to high school.

Teachers thought that Albert was lazy and not very smart, but they were wrong. Albert studied by himself and became one of the world's greatest scientists.

CHAPTER THREE

HARD TIMES

Albert went back to high school in Switzerland. He did very well at this school. The next year, he went to the **Technical** (TEK-nik-ul) Institute to study math and science. He fell in love with a girl named Mileva Maric. She was a classmate in his physics class. Physics (FIZZ-icks) is the study of **matter** and **energy**.

Albert still only liked to work on subjects that interested him. His math teacher called him a "lazy dog." Even the physics teacher thought he was not a good student. He was not lazy, though. He liked to do the work by himself, not in the classroom. Albert passed all of the tests and completed college.

CHAPTER THREE

Once Albert finished college, he struggled to find a job. Here he is sometime after college.

16

He tried to find a teaching job, but no one wanted to hire him. He could only find short-term jobs. Finally Albert took a job in a **patent** (PAT-unt) office in Bern, Switzerland. The office job was exactly the kind of dull, boring job that Albert Einstein had said he would never take. It turned out to be what he needed. Because it was dull, his mind was free to work on his scientific ideas.

Albert's father died in 1902. In 1903 he married Mileva, the girl from his physics class. They had two sons.

In 1905, Albert earned another degree from the University of Zurich, called a doctorate (DOC-tor-it). Then he wrote four papers about light and energy. They were published in a very important German science magazine.

Albert finally found a job teaching at a University. Here he explains a lesson in physics to his students.

CHAPTER FOUR

FAME

Scientists all over Europe learned about Albert's theories (THEER-eez), but Albert's ideas were difficult to understand. His ideas were about the **universe**. Only scientists who were very good at math and physics could figure out what he was writing about. Universities all over Europe began to offer him jobs. In 1909 he began teaching at a University. Soon he was given other teaching jobs. This meant that Albert had to move his family from one place to another all of the time.

He finally accepted a full-time job at the University of Berlin in Germany. Mileva was tired of moving. She wanted to go back to Switzerland. Albert and Mileva divorced in 1919.

CHAPTER FOUR

Albert gave many speeches. It was difficult for people to understand what he was saying because he was so smart.

Albert continued to teach and study physics. One of Albert's theories was that light was bent by gravity (GRAV-uh-tee). Gravity is the invisible force that causes objects to fall towards the ground when you drop them. In 1919 there was an eclipse (ee-KLIPS) of the sun. The moon came between the earth and the sun. Scientists took photographs of starlight during the eclipse. The photos showed that Albert was right! The gravity from the sun caused the light to bend.

Albert was nominated for the Nobel Prize in physics. The Nobel Prizes are the most important awards in the world. He won the prize in 1922. It took many years to win because many people did not understand his theories.

Albert became a very famous scientist. Thousands of people wanted to hear him speak. But they couldn't understand his ideas. When he spoke in front of an audience, he would speak for five minutes then he would say that people who did not want to hear more could leave. Only a few would stay.

Albert and his wife, Elsa, travel to the United States to escape war in Europe. Here they look out of a train window while traveling through Chicago.

CHAPTER FIVE

GOING TO AMERICA

Albert Einstein was a pacifist (PASS-uh-fist), a person who is against war. In the 1930s, a few years before World War II began, a man named Adolf Hitler gained power in Germany. Hitler hated people of other religions, especially of the Jewish religion. Albert was Jewish.

Albert knew that if he stayed in Germany he would be killed. Not only was he Jewish, but Adolf Hitler and his army hated Jewish scientists even more. In 1933, Albert and his second wife, Elsa, moved to America. Albert's sister Maja soon joined them. People in the United States welcomed the Einsteins. President Franklin D. Roosevelt (ROOS-uh-velt) invited them to dinner.

CHAPTER FIVE

Once he got to America, Albert wanted to become an American citizen. Here he is being sworn in as a citizen.

Princeton (PRINS-ton) University offered Albert a good job. He also lectured at other universities. In 1940 Albert became a United States citizen.

Other scientists used Albert's theories to make a very dangerous bomb, called an atomic bomb. Albert did not know that the bomb was going to be used to kill people. It was dropped on Japan in 1945, killing 70,000 people. He heard about it on the radio.

This is the explosion of the atomic bomb dropped on Japan.

CHAPTER FIVE

Albert did many great things in his life. He kept working until he died.

GOING TO AMERICA

World War II ended soon afterward. Albert returned to his pacifist work. He told people how terrible atomic weapons were. He continued to work for peace. He also continued to work on his scientific theories.

Albert Einstein died at his home in Princeton, New Jersey on April 18, 1955. Albert's theories and ideas still live on today. They are studied in science classes everywhere. Albert was a great scientist who changed the world.

CHRONOLOGY

1879 Albert Einstein is born in Ulm, Germany on March 14
1895 Albert leaves school in Germany to live his family in Italy
1900 Albert graduates from the Technical Institute in Switzerland
1903 He works at the Swiss Patent Office and marries Mileva Maric
1905 An important science magazine publishes four of Albert's papers
1913 Albert becomes a professor at the University of Berlin
1922 Albert is awarded the Nobel Prize in Physics
1933 The Einstein family moves to the United States
1940 Albert becomes a U.S. citizen
1945 Atomic bomb dropped on Japanese cities and Albert returns to pacifist work
1955 Albert dies at home in Princeton on April 18

FIND OUT MORE

Books

Gomez, Rebecca. *Albert Einstein* (First Biographies). Edina, Minnesota: Abdo & Daughters, 2003.

Lepscky, Ibi. *Albert Einstein* (Famous People Series). Hauppauge, New York: Barrons Juveniles, 1993.

MacLeod, Elizabeth. *Albert Einstein: A Life of Genius.* Toronto: Kids Can Press, 2003.

Parker, Steve. *Albert Einstein and Relativity.* New York: Chelsea House Publishers, 1995.

Rau, Dana Meachen. *Albert Einstein* (Compass Point Early Biographies). Minneapolis: Compass Point Books, 2003.

Schaefer, Lois and Wyatt Schaefer. *Albert Einstein* (First Biographies). Farmington, Michigan: Pebble Press, 2003.

Wishinsky, Frieda. *What's the Matter with Albert? A Story of Albert Einstein.* Toronto: Maple Tree Press, 2002.

FIND OUT MORE

On the Internet:

Albert Einstein
http://www-gap.dcs.st-and.ac.uk/~history/Mathematicians/Einstein.html

Einstein—Image and Impact
http://www.aip.org/history/einstein/

Nova Online—Einstein Revealed
http://www.pbs.org/wgbh/nova/einstein/

GLOSSARY

energy (EN-ur-jee)—light and heat

graduate (GRAD-juw-ate)—to complete school

matter (MAT-tur)—anything you can touch

patent (PAT-unt)—legal protection for an invention

technical (TECK-nuh-kul)—skill used in a science

universe (YUW-nuh-vurs)—all of space

university (yuw-nuh-VURS-uh-tee)—a school after high school

INDEX

Army 9
Doctorate 17
Gravity 21
Einstein, Albert
    birth of 5
    death of 27
    jobs 17, 19
    schooling of 9, 11, 13, 15
Einstein, Elsa (second wife) 23
Einstein, Herman 5, 11, 17
Einstein, Pauline 5
Einstein, Maja 7, 23
Hitlet, Adolf 23
Maric, Mileva (first wife) 15, 17, 19
Nobel Prize 21
Patent 17
Physics 15, 17, 19
Princeton University 25
Roosevelt, Franklin D. 23
Technical Institute 15
Theories 19, 21, 25, 27
World War II 23, 25, 27